My Doggy Duffy

To _____

From _____

Date _____

"My Doggy Duffy." Written by Sophia Juliet. Illustrated by Lourdes M. Devers.
ISBN# 978-0-578-33494-3. It can be purchased in bulk from Amazon or as an e-book.
If you wish to purchase hardcover books of this series for your collection, go to:
www.intuitkidspress@gmail.com or thesenseskids@gmail.com. (Doggy Duffy, adventure
book of animals, Christian children's books, love and compassion books).

Library of Congress number in publication data.
Published by Intuit Kids Press, South Carolina, USA.

My Doggy Duffy
and The
Day He Ran Away

Story by Sophia Juliet and Lourdes M. Devers

Pictures by Lourdes M. Devers

Hello, I'm Sophia. I have a doggy. He's white and fluffy, and his name is Duffy. He's a poodle you know, but Let me tell you more about him.

He is the best dog ever. He sleeps beside my bed. I feed him good food and clean water. I give him warm baths, and brush his fluffy, white fur.

He gives me puppy kisses, guards the house, and makes me laugh. Well, most of the time anyway; except for this one day.

I was running a fever and didn't go to school. I stayed home all bundled up in my pink pajamas and fuzzy bunny slippers. It had been raining hard for a couple of days. That day the weather looked as miserable as I felt.

Duffy needed to go outside. Arf! Arf!
He barked urgently! So I opened the back door
of the house. What I didn't know then, but found
out later, was that the wind had flung open the gate.

What dog could resist the temptation to wander
out and explore the streets? At least that's what I
figured out a while later when I went to look for him
and, to my surprise, the gate was opened, and in the
yard, there was no Duffy!

You can just imagine how I felt. I looked for him
everywhere! I went up and down the streets. Then
suddenly, I caught a glimpse of Duffy.

There he is! I shouted, as my heart jumps inside my chest. I see this little white doggy crossing the dangerous street as cars and trucks pass by him.

I run toward him as I scream hysterically. "Duffy! Duffy!" But the car noises are loud, and he doesn't hear me.

He didn't even look in my direction. Instead, he disappeared between the cars, then between the houses. I kept searching but, to my great despair, no Duffy.

"I can't find Duffy. He just ran away!"
I told my neighbors who gathered to find out
what was happening.

"Oh no!" said one of them.

"That's terrible!" said another.

"Sophia, is that why you are running around
outside in your pink pajamas and fuzzy bunny
slippers?" crooned the neighborhood granny, as
she peered over her glasses.

"Don't worry, Sophia, we will help you find
Duffy," said a mom, as she tried to reassure me.

Soon, all my neighbors pitched in
to search for Duffy. They looked
everywhere up and down the streets.

Then all of a sudden-*ZOOM!* A big
noisy truck barked right past us - I mean
it was a barking truck - I mean it was full
of barking dogs! Bark! Bark! Woof! Woof!
Yap! Yap! Arf! Arf!

"Duffy is in that truck!" I shouted.
"I would know that bark anywhere!"

We ran after that truck waving our arms.
"Stop! Stop!" my neighbors yelled.
"You got her Duffy!"

"Stop!" I cried, "you've got my ..." but the truck was going too fast, and the driver was too far away to hear us. Then the van disappeared down the street. I groaned a sigh of regret. Agh!

More parents gathered at the bus stop waiting to pick up their childen. Suddenly, around the corner came the school bus I always ride on.

It stopped to drop off the children.

"Sophia, why are you running outside
in your pink pajamas and fuzzy bunny slippers?"
asked the bus driver.

"I've been sick with a fever," I replied.

"But worse than that, I lost my doggy Duffy!"
I was sobbing as I answered.

"And worse than that," sniff, "now a truck is
taking him to the dog pound!"

"Yeah," agreed the neighbors.

"They are taking him to the dog pound!"

As if the sky wanted to cry with us,
it began to rain hard again. That's when the
bus driver said,

"Well what are we waiting for? C'mon guys, hop on the bus. Let's go get Duffy!" So, we all squeezed into the bus; the bus driver, the neighbors, their children, and me. We were soaked, could hardly move, and with the rain we could barely see outside.

"I will try to hurry as fast as I can," said the bus driver as she zoomed away. Then a dad shouted.

"The dog pound closes at 5 o'clock."

"We might be able to make it," said a mom. Well, the bus drove as fast as it could, until we got to the big town.

So instead of hurrying, the bus slowly crept up and down the streets, heading east and heading west. We were breaking out in a sweat!

"What if Duffy does not recognize me, and gives me the cold shoulder?" I wondered.
"What if someone adopts Duffy and I never see him again?" I sighed.
"What if he is happier with his new owner, and when he sees me, he attacks me like a killer dog? Oh, nooo!"

Then my pounding heart reminded me: *"Trust in the Lord with all your heart. Don't lean on your own understanding. In all thy ways acknowledge Him, and He will direct your path."* Proverbs 3:5-6.
Oh! I felt so much better!

It was five minutes before 5 o'clock and we were still not there! Oh my! Every traffic signal was a red light.

With just seconds to go before closing time, we still were not there!

We counted down 10, 9, 8, 7...that's when the bus suddenly screeched to a halt in front of the dog pound.

The driver flung open the bus door, pushhh, then we dashed into the dog pound entrance. Trying to get through at once all of us got jammed. Ugh! Ugh!

The dog pound keeper turned and said, "Wait! Wait! What's going on there? Step back!" Well, once we were inside, he asked. "Now, what seems to be the problem?"

Everybody started to talk at the same time. "Bla! Bla! Bla!"

"Wait! Wait!" shouted the pound keeper, as he placed his hands over his ears. "One at a time please!"

That's when I raised my hand and stepped forward. Tears filled my eyes, and it was hard to talk past the lump in my throat, but I explained what happened.

"My doggy is the best dog ever. He is white and fluffy and his name is Duffy. I searched for him everywhere, but to my great sadness," sniff, "no Duffy.

Then we saw the dog pound truck pass by us. I knew Duffy was inside. I would know that bark anywhere Please, give him back..." I pleaded.

The bus driver, the neighbors, and their children all agreed. "Yes please, give him back!"

"Hmm. Wait right here for a moment. Let me see what I can do," the pound keeper said.
Well, that was the longest "moment" ever!

All my worries and doubtful thoughts came rushing right back to me.

My heart pounded. What if? What if? What if? I felt sweaty, yet the quiet voice whispered, "Trust Me. Trust Me. Trust Me!"

After that I felt peaceful and hopeful. I needed and wanted to trust and believe that things would turn out good. So I waited patiently, or tried to.

Finally, the pound keeper came back holding a dog in his arms. I looked at it, but it didn't look anything like my Duffy!

I mean, I'm not trying to complain, but this dog's body was dark gray, and his face was brown, as if he'd been eating dirt!

I thought I was having a nightmare. I burst into tears with the thought of never ever seeing my Duffy again. Sniff.

My bottom lip trembled, and my legs felt weak. I slowly sank to the floor. While I pouted, the pound keeper placed the dog down on the floor.

I opened my arms and said, "Now what?" That's when this dog charges toward me like a killer dog! He knocks me over.

"EEEKKK!" I screamed.

While I'm on the floor, he starts to wag his little tail and lick my face! Then he barks, "Arf! Arf!"

"He barks just like Duffy!" I screamed, wiping the tears from my eyes. "I know that bark anywhere!"

"Woo-hoo!" everyone cheered and clapped, including the pound keeper. I held my Duffy out and laughed. "You surely are my grubby doggy. Just look at you! And your face is so dirty. Have you been eating dirt too?"

"You are going to need a long warm bath, young man!" I scolded Duffy. "Then I will wrap you in my special blanket," I said softly, as I held my doggy close. Needless to say, he kissed my face and soon I had mud on it, on my hands, my pink pajamas, and my fuzzy bunny slippers!

"Sophia, you are going to need a bath too,
young lady!" said the neighborhood granny,
as she peered over her glasses.

"Yes, I will," I replied. Then we all laughed.
I snuggled Duffy in my arms and said,"Thank you,
everyone, for helping me find Duffy!"

"You are welcome," they all answered,
as they came closer to get a better look at Duffy.
Then someone added,"That was quite a school
bus ride we had, coming over to get your Duffy."
Agreeing, we all laughed some more.

We got back on the bus. The dog pound keeper waved goodbye as we droved away.

I looked out the window and the sky was clear. The late afteernoon sun was shining. I thanked God for His goodness, and hugged my doggy Duffy closed to my heart. Once home mom and dad were glad we were safe.

"Sophia whatever happened to your fever?" asked mom. "What fever? I feel perfectly fine." I replied as my parents looked at each other with raised brows.

I went on to give Duffy a bath, and to wrap him up in my very special blanket.

"Look dad, look mom, Duffy is eating his food so fast. He must be so hungry," I said as they looked on.

Next, I brushed his fur. He was so tired he went right to sleep on my lap. I could tell he was glad to be home.

The next day I took Duffy for a short walk on a leash. We played in the yard, then stayed home for the rest of the day.

My dad made sure the fence had a good lock so Duffy would never ever run away again. Would he ever run away again? Hmm.

Do you know someone who loves you even more than Sophia loves her doggy Duffy? Yeshua loves you! (That's Jesus' Hebrew name).

When we run away from Him, He goes out to look for us. When He finds us, Yeshua (Jesus) receives us with open arms, gives us a warm bath (to cleanse us from all sin), then wraps us up in His Holy Spirit special blanket of love and grace.

Luke 19:10 The Lord came to seek and save the lost.
John 15:3 Now you are clean with the word I have spoken to you.
Ephesians 4:7 But in each one of us Grace has been given as appointed by Yeshua (Jesus).

Thank Him always for His goodness.

On sale now at: Amazon

A Silly Worm

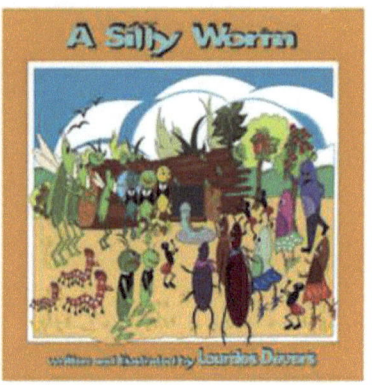

An easy-to-read book of rhymes about a worm looking bug who is insulted and bullied by all the other insects in his bug-town. Little did they know this was no ordinary worm!
by **Lourdes M. Devers**

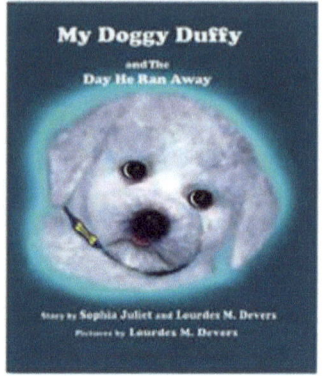

My Doggy Duffy

Exciting Adventure of the day Duffy ran away!
by **Sophia Juliet**

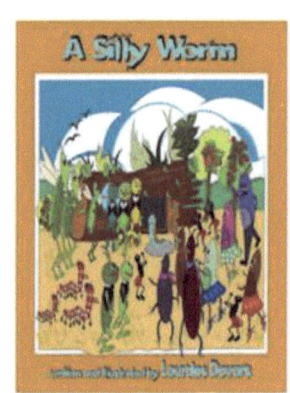

e-book

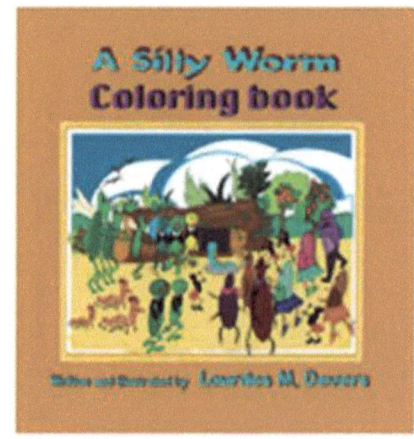

A Silly Worm
coloring book

Coming Soon!

#2 series

My Doggy Duffy
and the Day He
Ran Away Again on
Christmas Eve
by
Sophia Juliet

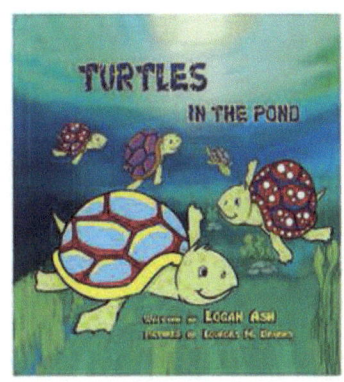

*Come along and
sing our song*
*Turtles in
the Pond*
by
Logan Ash

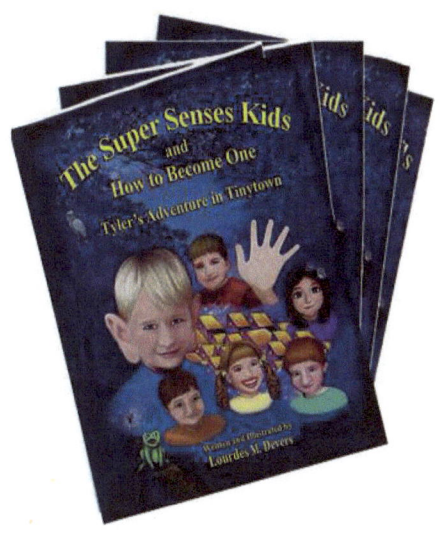

5 Series

The Super Senses Kids
and How to Become One
by
Lourdes M. Devers

For more inspiring stories visit us at:

thesenseskids.com

intuitkidspress.com.

Amazon.com

Contact us at:
thesenseskids@gmail.com

intuitkidspress@gmail.com

It is our pleasure to write inspirational children's books for all of you. So keep on reading our books, and we will keep on writng them. Join, support, and like us on social media. Thank you.

www.ingramcontent.com/pod-product-compliance
Lightning Source LLC
Chambersburg PA
CBHW040959170626
46815CB00002B/75